THE MLB FAN'S GUIDE

12 REASONS TO LOVE THE DETROIT TIGERS

by David Aretha

12 STORY LIBRARY

www.12StoryLibrary.com

12-Story Library is an imprint of Peterson Publishing Company and Press Room Editions.

Produced for 12-Story Library by Red Line Editorial

Photographs ©: Carlos Osorio/AP Images, cover, 1, 7; Jeff Chiu/AP Images, 4; Tony Dejak/AP Images, 5, 28; Gary Paul Lewis/Shutterstock Images, 8; Scott W. Grau/Icon Sportswire/AP Images, 9, 29; Duane Burleson/AP Images, 11; Linda Parton/Shutterstock Images, 12; Scott Boehm/AP Images, 13; Tigers Archives/AP Images, 14; Bain News Service/Library of Congress, 15; AP Images, 17, 19, 25; Bettmann/Corbis, 21, 23; Ray Stubblebine/AP Images, 22; Ron Heflin/AP Images, 24; Elise Amendola/AP Images, 26; Amy Sancetta/AP Images, 27

ISBN
978-1-63235-211-8 (hardcover)
978-1-63235-238-5 (paperback)
978-1-62143-263-0 (hosted ebook)

Library of Congress Control Number: 2015934316

Printed in the United States of America
Mankato, MN
October, 2015

TABLE OF CONTENTS

1

TIGERS RULE THE CENTRAL DIVISION

Catcher Alex Avila threw off his mask. He looked up at the sky. When the pop-up landed in his mitt, his Detroit Tigers had beaten the Minnesota Twins on the last day of the 2014 regular season. Tigers players ran onto the field. The crowd went wild. With the victory, the Tigers won the American League (AL) Central Division title for the fourth consecutive season.

From 2011 to 2014, the Tigers had plenty of star power. Miguel Cabrera led the league in batting average three times—and blasted 143 home runs. Pitcher Justin Verlander went 24–5 in 2011. Fireballer

Tigers pitcher Justin Verlander delivers a pitch in the 2012 World Series.

Max Scherzer was 21–3 in 2013. Designated hitter Victor Martinez batted .335 in 2014.

The Tigers made it to the World Series in only one of those years, 2012. In that year's Fall Classic, the San Francisco Giants defeated the Tigers in four straight games. Still, winning four straight division titles is special.

Victor Martinez follows through on a home run during a 2014 game.

91.5

Average wins per season for the Tigers from 2011 to 2014.

- The Tigers won the AL Central Division every year from 2011 to 2014.
- They won the AL Division Series in 2011, 2012, and 2013.
- They won the AL Championship Series (ALCS) in 2012.

THINK ABOUT IT

The Tigers were one of baseball's best teams during the regular season from 2011 to 2014. However, they didn't win a World Series during that time. Would you still consider those to be successful seasons? Explain why or why not.

2

MIGGY SUPPLIES THE POWER

During batting practice, Tigers superstar Miguel Cabrera likes to play a game called Around the World. First he'll hit a ball into the right field seats. Then he'll go deep to center field—and then to left! During games, Cabrera loves to jokes around. He smiles and laughs with teammates, opponents, and sometimes even fans. It's easy to be relaxed when you hit as well as "Miggy."

"If he stays healthy," said Tigers pitcher Justin Verlander, "I don't see any reason why he can't be the best hitter of all time."

Since joining the Tigers in 2008, Cabrera has been the game's greatest slugger. He has batted .325 while averaging 36 home runs and 121 runs batted in (RBIs). With the Florida Marlins and then Detroit, he had topped 100 RBIs for 11 straight seasons through 2014. The Major League Baseball (MLB) record is 13.

THE KING IS CROWNED

Late during the 2012 season, Tigers fans began wearing hats with three crowns on them. They represented the Triple Crown that Miguel Cabrera was about to win. A hitter wins the Triple Crown if he leads the AL or National League (NL) in batting average, home runs, and RBIs. In 2012, Miggy led the AL with a .330 average, 44 homers, and 139 RBIs. He became the first Triple Crown winner in either league since 1967.

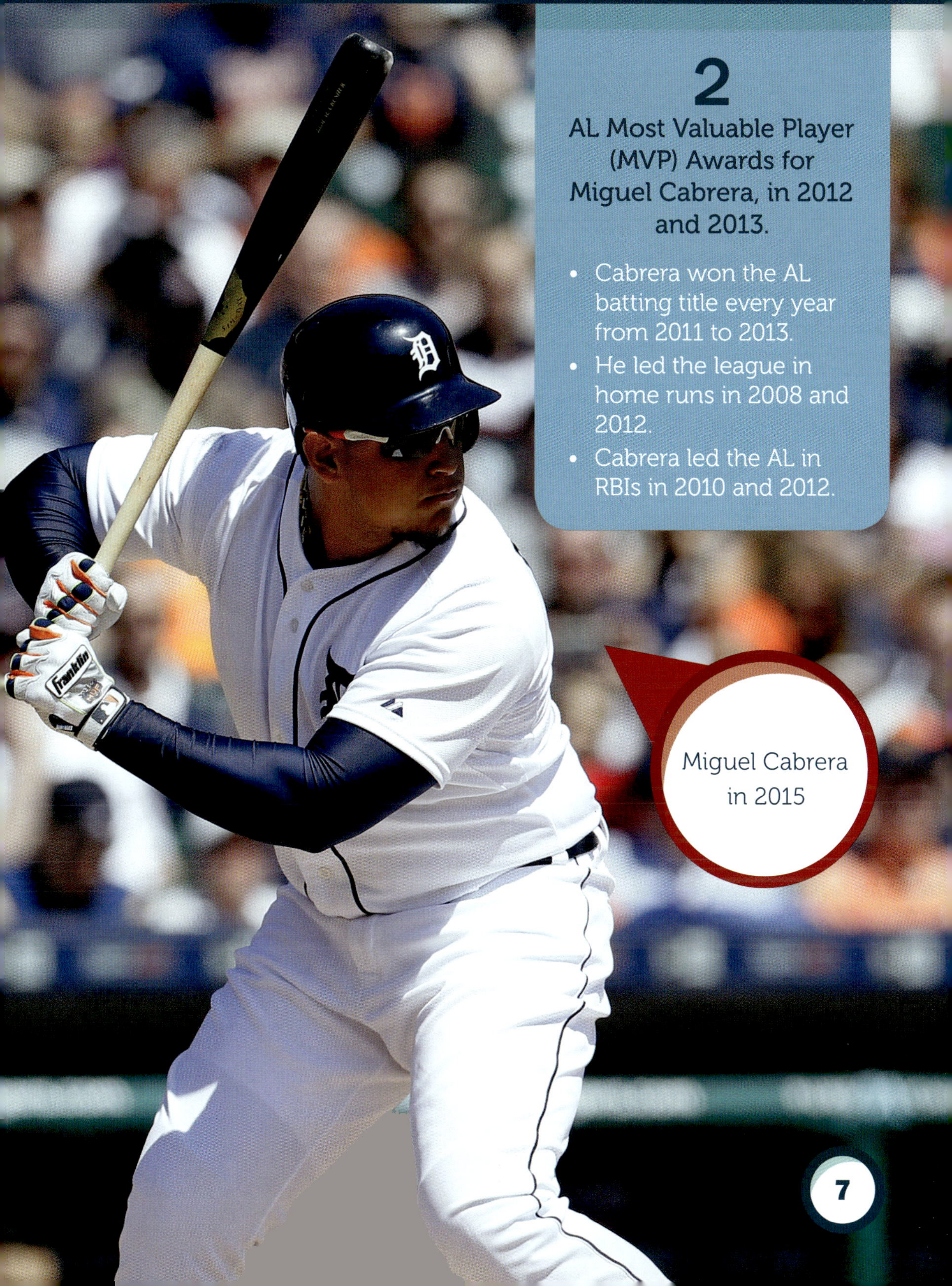

2

AL Most Valuable Player (MVP) Awards for Miguel Cabrera, in 2012 and 2013.

- Cabrera won the AL batting title every year from 2011 to 2013.
- He led the league in home runs in 2008 and 2012.
- Cabrera led the AL in RBIs in 2010 and 2012.

Miguel Cabrera in 2015

3

COMERICA PARK IS DETROIT'S HAPPY PLACE

In the 1990s, Detroiters started a movement called "Save Tiger Stadium." They even circled the ballpark and hugged it. Tiger Stadium dated back to 1912. Fans loved the cozy ballpark. They cherished the wonderful memories that had been created there. They didn't want to see it go. Unfortunately, Tiger Stadium was falling apart.

In 2000, Comerica Park became the team's new home. It's a state-of-the-art ballpark. Fans have a clear view of the field and the downtown skyline. Comerica Park has several unusual features. For one, a strip of dirt runs from the pitcher's mound to the batter's box. Outside, massive, menacing Tiger statues greet the fans. Kids can even ride a tiger-themed merry-go-round.

Tiger statues greet fans outside Comerica Park.

Comerica Park offers great views of downtown Detroit.

Fans flock to Comerica Park in huge numbers. In a good year, more than 3 million fans attend a Tigers game at Comerica Park.

FRIENDLY PAWS

Since 1995, Paws has been a regular at Tigers home games. The mascot can often be found prowling the stands, waving a Tigers flag or high-pawing boys and girls. Paws is still a cub at heart. He lists fantasy baseball and collecting baseball cards among his hobbies.

88

Seasons in which the Tigers played at Tiger Stadium, from 1912 to 1999.

- Tiger Stadium was known as Navin Field and Briggs Stadium before 1961.
- Comerica Park opened in 2000.
- The Tigers drew a team-record 3,202,645 fans in 2008.

4

VERLANDER BLOWS HITTERS AWAY

Most fans expected the Tigers to improve in 2006. Few expected them to win 24 more games than they did in 2005, though. Pitcher Justin Verlander played a big role in that improvement. The team had picked him second overall in the 2004 MLB draft. In 2006, the rookie made the team as Detroit's fifth starter. Before long, the Virginia native was their ace.

Verlander overwhelmed hitters with his 100 mile-per-hour (161 km/h) fastball. His 3.63 earned-run average (ERA) led the team. And his 17 wins tied for the team lead. Behind the hotshot rookie, the Tigers made a run all the way to the World Series. Few were surprised when he was named the AL Rookie of the Year.

Verlander's best was yet to come. From 2006 to 2014, he won 152

17

Average wins per season for Justin Verlander from 2006 to 2014.

- Verlander was named to six All-Star Games in that time.
- He led the AL in strikeouts in 2009, 2011, and 2012.
- Verlander became only the 10th pitcher to win Cy Young and MVP awards in the same season.

THINK ABOUT IT

What qualities do you look for in your favorite player? How much do you care if the player is friendly? Or is the player's performance on the field all that matters?

games and lost only 87. He led the league in strikeouts three times. He also threw two no-hitters and starred in the postseason. Verlander's best season was 2011. He led the league with 24 wins, a 2.40 ERA, and 250 strikeouts. That year, he won the AL Cy Young Award and the AL MVP Award. Usually the MVP Award goes to a hitter.

All the while, Verlander represented the Tigers with class. He's a leader in the clubhouse. He's naturally friendly and often smiling (except when he's on the mound). Plus, he contributes to charitable causes, particularly those that support military veterans.

Justin Verlander follows through on a pitch in a 2013 game.

5

THE D STANDS FOR DETROIT

Since 1904, the Tigers have worn the Olde English D on their home uniforms. The letter has come to symbolize the team and its city. “There are very few things you can count on today that have not changed,” said University of Detroit–Mercy professor Michael Bernacchi. “The Olde English logo has not. Whether it’s worn on the hat or on the uniform, you instantly—if you know anything about sports—know who it stands for.”

But the Tigers are not just Detroit’s team. People from all over Michigan cheer on the Tigers. On summer evenings in the Upper Peninsula, perhaps while fishing in Lake Superior, fans can be found listening to Tigers games on the radio.

A Tigers jersey on the Spirit of Detroit monument in downtown Detroit

The Olde English D on a Tigers hat

Ernie Harwell broadcast games every year but one from 1960 to 2002. When a player hit a foul ball into the stands, he would think of a city name in Michigan. "A lady from Kalamazoo caught that one," he'd say. On the next foul ball, "A man from Traverse City grabbed that souvenir."

Tigers pride: In Michigan, it's everywhere.

WHO WANTS PIZZA?

If your family buys Little Caesars pizza, they're contributing in a small way to the success of the Tigers. That's because Little Caesars owner Mike Ilitch also owns Detroit's baseball team (and its hockey team, the Red Wings). The team's previous owner also was a pizza guy. Tom Monaghan owned the Tigers from 1983 to 1992. He founded Domino's.

1

Tigers minor league team in Michigan. The Class A West Michigan Whitecaps play in Comstock Park.

- The Tigers formed in 1901.
- They have won more than 9,000 games.
- The Olde English D symbolizes the team.

6

FIERY COBB HITS AND HITS AND HITS

Ty Cobb always wanted to be the best. On the baseball field, that meant playing with ferocity. As teammate Sam Crawford said, Cobb played each game as if he "was fighting the Civil War." When that intensity was combined with Cobb's skills, the results were extraordinary.

Cobb led the AL in hitting every season from 1907 to 1915. He batted .420 in 1911 and .409 the following season. His career average of .366 is the greatest in major league history. Moreover, he set MLB records (since broken) for career hits (4,189), runs (2,246), and stolen bases (897).

Cobb played in an era before home runs were common. But when he wanted, he could hit for power, too. Cobb led the AL with nine home runs in 1909. Later, in 1925, Cobb wanted to prove a point. Babe Ruth was becoming a star by hitting home runs. Cobb believed

Ty Cobb (right) was known for his aggressive playing style.

Ruth's power was overrated. So Cobb hit five home runs over two games. Then he went back to his preferred style of base hits and blazing around the base paths.

"He was the greatest all-time ballplayer," said Casey Stengel, who played in the same era as Cobb. "That guy was superhuman."

The movie *Cobb* portrayed Cobb as a grouch in his old age. However, he was also a charitable man. He donated his fortune to fund Cobb Memorial Hospital in Georgia as well as the Cobb Educational Fund.

Ty Cobb shown around 1910

3

Seasons in which Ty Cobb batted at least .400.

- Cobb, who was from Georgia, was nicknamed "The Georgia Peach."
- He became the first MLB player to collect 4,000 hits.
- He led the AL in hits eight times and stolen bases six times.

THINK ABOUT IT

Ty Cobb was one of baseball's best hitters ever. However, he could also have a bad temper. He often fought with fans, opponents, and even teammates. Would you want Cobb on your team? Explain why or why not.

7

GREENBERG HOMERS AGAINST HITLER

Hank Greenberg was the first great Jewish baseball player. A mighty slugger, he put up astounding numbers for the Tigers. In 1934, he drilled 63 doubles. That ranks fourth most all-time. He drove in 170 runs in 1935. His 183 RBIs in 1937 is the third-most ever. In 1938, he blasted 58 home runs. That was two shy of Babe Ruth's MLB record at the time.

While Greenberg rose to fame in Detroit, horror descended upon the Jews of Europe. Germany's Nazi Party, led by Adolf Hitler, was beginning to oppress the Jewish citizens of Europe. They believed Jews were inferior human beings. And during World War II (1939–1945), the Nazis and their accomplices killed approximately 6 million Jews. As a ballplayer, Greenberg tried to show hateful people that Jews were not inferior. "I came to feel that if I, as a Jew, hit a home run, I was hitting one against Hitler," Greenberg said.

But "Hammerin' Hank" did more than just hit home runs. In 1941, he became the first star ballplayer to enlist in the army during World War II. He served four years. When he returned in 1945, he led the Tigers to the World Series title.

331

Home runs Hank Greenberg hit during his career.

- Greenberg won the AL MVP Award in 1935 and 1940.
- His 58 homers in 1938 set a team record.
- He has Detroit's top four seasons for RBIs.

Hank Greenberg follows through on a swing in 1940.

8

TIGERS ARE GREAT IN '68

The city of Detroit suffered through a terrible summer in 1967. Anger between black citizens and white police officers escalated into a race riot. More than 40 people were killed. The success of the Tigers in 1968 helped bring some peace and happiness back to the city.

Fun-loving pitcher Denny McLain led the way. He won 31 games. That was the most by an MLB pitcher since 1931. No pitcher has won 30 games since. The Tigers went 103–59. That was the best record in the AL. The playoffs didn't yet exist. So the Tigers advanced directly to the World Series.

In the Fall Classic, Detroit trailed the St. Louis Cardinals three games to one. That's when pitcher Mickey Lolich came to the rescue. He won the next game 5–3. Then the Tigers routed the Cardinals 13–1 in Game 6. In Game 7 in St. Louis, Detroit's Jim Northrup slammed a two-run triple, and Lolich won again, 4–1.

"We didn't give up," said Tigers slugger Gates Brown. "Just like the city."

7

Games needed for the Tigers to beat the Chicago Cubs in the 1945 World Series.

- Detroit pitcher Hal Newhouser went 25–9 and won a second straight AL MVP Award in 1945.
- Newhouser won Games 5 and 7 of the World Series.
- Detroit cruised in the final game to defeat the Cubs 9–3.

Mickey Lolich pitches for the Tigers in the 1968 World Series.

WORLD SERIES CHAMPIONS

Prior to 1968, the Tigers won two World Series. The first was in 1935. The G-men powered Detroit. Hank Greenberg (168 RBIs), Goose Goslin (111), and Charlie Gehringer (108) led the way. Detroit played the Chicago Cubs in the World Series. The Tigers clinched the title on Goslin's walk-off single in the ninth inning of Game 6. Detroit beat the Cubs again in the 1945 World Series.

9

KALINE BELOVED AS "MR. TIGER"

In 1969, the Tigers offered Al Kaline a salary of $100,000. He turned it down. He thought it was too much.

"I don't feel that I am worthy of such a salary," he said.

Well, he was plenty worthy. Kaline joined the Tigers out of high school in 1953. He never played in the minor leagues. In 1955, Kaline won the AL batting title (.340) at age 20. "Mr. Tiger" played 22 seasons with Detroit. He made the All-Star team 15 times.

Kaline could both hit and field. In the batter's box, he fell one homer shy of becoming the first AL player with 3,000 hits and 400 home runs. In right field, he played the position to perfection, winning 10 Gold Glove Awards.

Throughout his career, Kaline behaved like a gentleman. That was the only way he knew how to be.

"I have always served baseball to the best of my ability," he said. "Never have I deliberately done anything to discredit the game, the Tigers, or my family."

The Tigers retired Kaline's uniform No. 6. Fans still call him Mr. Tiger. The classy right fielder remains one of the most beloved players in team history.

THINK ABOUT IT

In 2000, the Tigers unveiled a statue of Al Kaline outside Comerica Park. Which current Tigers player should someday have his statue at the ballpark? List three reasons to support your choice.

3,007

Hits by Al Kaline over his 22 seasons with the Tigers.

- Kaline holds the Tigers' career record with 399 home runs.
- He was inducted into the Baseball Hall of Fame in 1980, on his first opportunity.

Al Kaline waits for a pitch in a 1974 game.

10

"WE WANT THE BIRD!"

The 1975 Tigers were the worst team in baseball. They lost 102 games. Fans had little to cheer about. Then, in 1976, "The Bird" flew in.

Rookie pitcher Mark "The Bird" Fidrych looked like Big Bird on the kids TV show *Sesame Street.* He had long, curly, golden hair. Plus he was a fun-loving goofball. On the

Mark Fidrych pitches during a 1976 game.

mound, he got on his knees and smoothed the dirt. While pitching, he actually talked to the baseball. After victories, he shook everyone's hand.

The Bird wasn't just a fun character. He was really good. Fidrych won 19 games in 1976 and lost only nine. He started for the AL in the All-Star Game. Tigers fans adored him. They packed Tiger Stadium when he pitched. If he won the game, they chanted, "We want The Bird! We want The Bird." When he responded by waving his cap, fans roared again.

Sadly, the magic lasted only one summer. In spring training in 1977, Fidrych hurt his knee while fooling around on the field. He later hurt his shoulder. Due to injuries, he won only 10 more games in his career.

Mark Fidrych poses with Big Bird in 1976.

2.34

Mark Fidrych's AL-leading ERA in 1976.

- Fidrych also led the AL with 24 complete games.
- He was the 1976 AL Rookie of the Year.

11

TIGERS ROAR IN '84

For a while in 1984, the Tigers looked like the greatest baseball team ever. In fact, they became the first MLB club to open a season at 35–5. They finished at 104–58 and breezed to the World Series.

Manager Sparky Anderson ran a disciplined team. "My way or the highway" was his motto. He made the most of a talented roster. Pitchers Jack Morris and Dan Petry won 37 games between them. Reliever Willie Hernandez recorded 32 saves and won the AL MVP Award. Catcher Lance Parrish and outfielder Kirk Gibson combined for 60 home runs.

After sweeping the Kansas City Royals in the ALCS, the Tigers roared to the World Series. Detroit led the San Diego Padres three games to one. Excitement grew in Game 5. In the eighth inning, Detroit led 5–4 at Tiger Stadium when Gibson came to the plate. The fiery slugger blasted a three-run homer deep to right. He pumped his fists in the air. The Tigers won 8–4 to clinch the World Series championship.

Pitcher Willie Hernandez (left) and catcher Lance Parrish celebrate the Tigers' win in the 1984 World Series.

6

Tigers players on the 1984 AL All-Star team.

- In 1984, Tigers closer Willie Hernandez became the seventh player to win the Cy Young and MVP awards in one season.
- Hernandez recorded a then-record 32 consecutive saves that season.

WHITAKER AND TRAMMELL

Lou Whitaker played second base for the Tigers from 1977 to 1995. "Sweet Lou" turned double plays with shortstop Alan Trammell all 19 seasons. In the history of the game, no second baseman and shortstop played together longer than Whitaker and Trammell. Each could swing the bat—they had 4,734 hits and 429 homers between them. Both were outstanding fielders, winning a combined seven Gold Glove Awards. In sum, they were named to 11 All-Star Games, with each going in 1984.

Shortstop Alan Trammell snags a grounder during the 1984 World Series.

12

TIGERS STIR UP MAGIC IN 2006

From 1989 to 2005, Tigers fans had little to cheer about. The team never contended for the playoffs. It hit rock bottom in 2003. The Tigers lost an AL-record 119 games. Everyone from comedian Jay Leno to TV's *The Simpsons* poked fun at them.

In 2006, everything changed. New manager Jim Leyland arrived. His disciplined approach helped change the attitude within the clubhouse. Some players had big seasons, too. Rookie pitcher Justin Verlander won 17 games. So did 41-year-old veteran Kenny Rogers. Reliever Joel Zumaya fired a 104.8-mph (168.7 km/h) fastball. Outfielder Magglio Ordonez batted .298 with 104 RBIs.

The Tigers made the playoffs as a wild-card team. In the AL Division Series, they upset the New York Yankees. Players were so excited after the game that they celebrated with fans in the front rows. Detroit then won all four games against the Oakland Athletics in the ALCS.

Pitcher Kenny Rogers tips his cap to Tigers fans in the 2006 playoffs.

Ordonez's walk-off homer to left field in Game 4 electrified Comerica Park.

Only the World Series was a disappointment. The St. Louis Cardinals beat Detroit in five games. The Tigers may have had the jitters. They committed eight fielding errors, including five by their pitchers.

136

Consecutive days in which the Tigers led the AL Central Division, from May 16 to September 30.

- The Tigers fell to second place on the final day of the season.
- They still made the playoffs for the first time since 1987.

Magglio Ordonez celebrates a walk-off home run during the 2006 playoffs.

12 KEY DATES

1901
The Tigers are founded the same year as the AL begins.

1907
The Tigers begin a streak in which they reach the World Series for three years in a row. However, they lose all three.

1915
The Tigers' Ty Cobb leads the AL in hitting. It is the ninth consecutive year in which he does so.

1935
Hank Greenberg, Goose Goslin, and Charlie Gehringer—the G-men—lead the way as the Tigers win their first World Series. Goslin hits a walk-off single to win the Series in Game 6.

1945
Ten years after beating the Chicago Cubs in the World Series, the Tigers do it again. This time MVP pitcher Hal Newhouser leads the way, winning Games 5 and 7.

1968
One year after riots in Detroit, the Tigers give fans something to cheer about when they beat the St. Louis Cardinals in a thrilling World Series.

1976
Pitcher Mark "The Bird" Fidrych takes Detroit by storm. He wins 19 games and the AL Rookie of the Year Award.

1984
The Tigers run away with the AL pennant and beat the San Diego Padres in the World Series.

2000
Comerica Park opens in downtown Detroit. It replaces Tiger Stadium, which dated back to 1912, as the Tigers' home ballpark.

2006
Three years after losing an MLB-record 119 games, the Tigers reach the World Series. The playoff berth is their first since 1987.

2011
Tigers pitcher Justin Verlander becomes just the 10th player to win the Cy Young and MVP awards in the same season. Former Detroit pitchers Willie Hernandez (1984) and Denny McLain (1968) also achieved that feat.

2012
Tigers slugger Miguel Cabrera wins the Triple Crown by leading the AL with a .330 average, 44 homers, and 139 RBIs.

GLOSSARY

ace
The best pitcher on a baseball team.

charitable
Helping of those in need.

draft
A system in which teams in a league take turns selecting players who are new to the league.

earned-run average (ERA)
A statistic that represents the number of runs a pitcher gives up over nine innings.

Gold Glove
An award given to the best defensive player at each position in each league every year.

mascot
A character who represents a team.

rookie
A first-year player.

saves
When a pitcher comes into a game and maintains a lead until the end of a game.

skyline
A view of a city's downtown buildings.

veteran
A player with a lot of experience.

walk-off
A play that ends a game.

wild-card
Playoff spots that go to the best teams that did not win their divisions.

FOR MORE INFORMATION

Books

Anderson, Jameson. *Miguel Cabrera.* Edina, MN: Abdo Publishing, 2014.

Gilbert, Sara. *Story of the Detroit Tigers.* Mankato, MN: Creative Education, 2012.

Savage, Jeff. *Justin Verlander.* Minneapolis: Lerner Publishing Group, 2013.

Stewart, Mark. *Detroit Tigers.* Chicago: Norwood House Press, 2012.

Websites

Detroit Tigers

www.detroit.tigers.mlb.com

MLB.com: Kids

mlb.mlb.com/mlb/kids

Tigers Kids

detroit.tigers.mlb.com/det/fan_forum/kids_index.jsp

INDEX

About the Author

A lifelong Tigers fan, David Aretha covered the team for *Sport Detroit Magazine*. As part of the Topps Company, he has written copy for hundreds of Tigers cards. Aretha has written and edited dozens of baseball books, including many for young readers. He served as editor for the book *Detroit Tigers: Yesterday & Today.*